# No Monster in the Closet

By Tasha Nathan

Illustrated By Peter M.R. Gosling

*AuthorHouse™*
*1663 Liberty Drive*
*Bloomington, IN 47403*
*www.authorhouse.com*
*Phone: 1-800-839-8640*

*Published by AuthorHouse  02/22/2012*

*ISBN:      978-1-4678-5377-4 (sc)*

authorHOUSE®

Dedicated to my parents and my dear friend, Ruth, who gave me the confidence to become the writer I always wanted to be.

Kyle was always scared. He was scared of going to school because he thought he wouldn't be as smart as the other students, so he never answered any questions the teacher asked the class.

He was scared of making friends because he thought that they wouldn't like to play with him, so he played by himself most of the time during recess. He was scared of making too much noise because he thought it would get him into trouble, so he stayed quiet all the time.

**B**ut there was one thing that scared Kyle more than anything else. Kyle was scared of the monster in the closet that came alive at night. Every night when his mom kissed him good night and turned off the lights, he always made sure that she remembered to turn the night light on before the room became dark.

"Kyle, you're a big boy; there are no such things as monsters," his mom would always say to him. But Kyle didn't care. He didn't think he could be brave enough to stay all alone in a dark room without any lights on.

You see, during the night, when the whole house was dark, and everyone was sleeping, the monster would start knocking on the closet door, and he roared to be let out.

**"ROARRRRRR! ROARRRRRRRRRRRR!"**

And when the roaring got really ferocious, he would leap out from the covers and hide under the bed.

As each night passed by, Kyle became more and more frightened as he thought of the monster coming out.

One night the monster became really crazy.

**"ROOOOAAAARRRR! LET ME OUT, OR I'LL EAT YOU!"** it shouted.

**SLAM!** Kyle jumped as the monster slammed into the door trying to open it.

**CRASH! SLAM! THUD!**
**CRASH! SLAM! THUD!**
**CRASH! SLAM! THUD!**
**CRASH! SLAM! THUD!**

**A**s the noise continued, Kyle began to cry. He tried to huddle as far away from the closet as possible. He finally scurried under the bed and covered his ears until the noise stopped. After a while the noise went away, and he fell asleep under the bed.

**T**he next morning, Kyle woke up to his mother calling him, "Kyle! Wake up sweetie."

He opened his eyes and saw his mother's worried face looking at him. He crawled out of from under the bed and into his mother's arms.

"Kyle why were you under the bed?" she asked.

"Because the monster was going to get me," he replied.

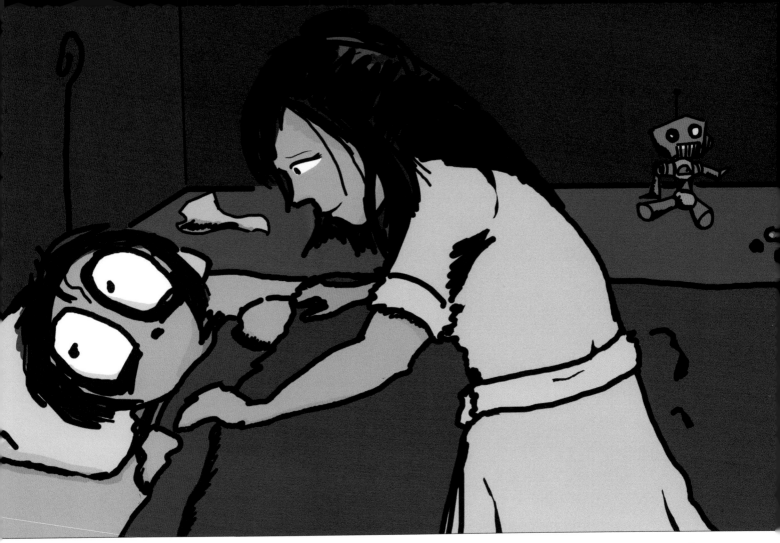

**K**yle's mom hugged him and said, "There are no monsters in the closet, Kyle. You have to stop thinking there are. Monsters only exist as long as you believe they exist."

"But it's so loud, Mom. It roars and slams against the door, and it said that it would eat me!" Kyle started crying again as he thought of the monster banging at the door. "Mommy, *please* can I sleep with you tonight?"

"Kyle, you can't be scared forever. The more you get scared, the more the monster becomes real. The only way to get rid of the monster is to be brave and face the monster. Then you'll see that there is no monster but only your fear that created the monster."

**K**yle thought about what his mother said the entire day. He thought about it as the teacher taught them in class; he thought about it as he played by himself at recess, and he thought about it during playtime.

**A**nd he kept on thinking about it as he brushed his teeth and got ready for bed.

**K**yle crawled under the covers and waited for the monster to start roaring. He waited and waited, and then he waited some more. There was still no noise from the closet. He waited for a long time, and just as he was about to fall asleep—

"Roooooooaaaarrrr! Let me out!

Let me out or I'll eat you!"

**K**yle jumped at the noise and hugged himself as the monster continued to yell. "It's only my imagination. It's only my imagination," he repeated to himself as he remembered what his mother said.

*I* *have to face the monster,* he thought, and so he took a deep breath and started to climbed out of bed…

"AAAAHHHH!" Kyle jumped back into bed and shook from fear.

"LET ME OUT!"

CRASH! SLAM! THUD!

**K**yle peered at the closet door through his covers. The door rattled as the monster tried to open to door.

Kyle closed his eyes and said, "I can do this; it's only my imagination. There are no such things as monster."

Taking a deep breath, Kyle jumped out of bed and slowly started walking towards the closet with shaky knees.

# "ROOOAARR!"

Kyle stood still. He was so scared he felt his knees knock together from fear. He really wanted to run back to his bed and hide under the covers, but he knew that if he did, the monster would never go away.

He continued walking until he stood right in front of the closet door.

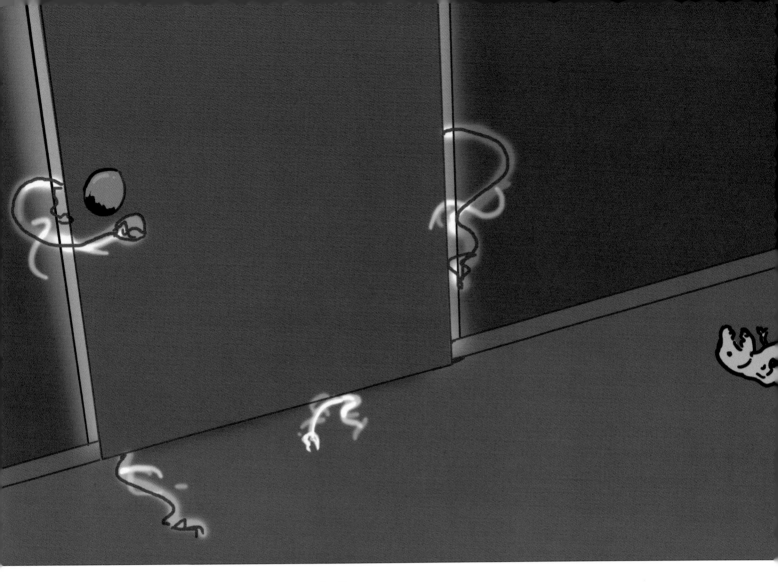

# CRASH! SLAM! THUD!

The door rattled and shook.

# "LET ME OUT! LET ME OUT!"

The monster cried out angrily.

**"YOU ARE NOT REAL!"** Kyle yelled at the monster, **"GO AWAY!"**

**"LET ME OUT! LET ME OUT!"** the monster continued to shout.

"I SAID YOU ARE NOT REAL!"

**A**nd with that, Kyle gathered up all of his courage and opened the closet door. He slowly looked inside and saw—

# **N**othing

There was nothing inside the closet.

Kyle looked in the corners of the closet, but there was no sign of the monster. He looked up at the ceiling; no monster there either. He looked all around inside the closet, but he found no monster. There was no monster in the closet.

Kyle sighed in relief, and his face broke into a big smile. He climbed back into his bed and went to sleep peacefully.

**A**fter his fear of monster went away, Kyle became much braver. Now when Kyle goes to school, he isn't afraid to raise his hand to answer the teacher's question.

**A**t recess time, he isn't afraid to go up to the other students and play with them.

**N**ow, whenever they have playtime, Kyle isn't afraid of making too much noise. Instead, he makes sure to make as much noise as possible.

**A**nd lastly, during bedtime, Kyle goes straight to bed and is never scared of monsters again.